FEEDING THE SHEEP

LEDA SCHUBERT   PICTURES BY ANDREA U'REN

Farrar Straus Giroux / New York

Text copyright © 2010 by Leda Schubert
Pictures copyright © 2010 by Andrea U'Ren
Distributed in Canada by D&M Publishers, Inc.
Color separations by Embassy Graphics
Printed in October 2009 in China by Toppan Leefung Printers Ltd.,
Dongguan City, Guangdong Province
Designed by Jay Colvin
First edition, 2010
10 9 8 7 6 5 4 3 2 1

www.fsgkidsbooks.com

Library of Congress Cataloging-in-Publication Data
Schubert, Leda.
    Feeding the sheep / Leda Schubert ; pictures by Andrea U'Ren.— 1st ed.
        p.   cm.
    Summary: In pictures and rhythmic text, a mother relates to her daughter all the steps
involved in making her a snug, wooly sweater, starting at the very beginning with feeding
the sheep.
    ISBN: 978-0-374-32296-0
    [1. Sheep—Fiction.   2. Weaving—Fiction.   3. Wool—Fiction.   4. Mothers and
daughters—Fiction.] I. U'Ren, Andrea, ill. II. Title.

PZ8.3.S378Fe 2010
[E]—dc22

                                                                        2007048843

To Phyllis Root —L.S.
For Sebastian Elias Healy —A.U.

"What are you doing?" the little girl asked.
"Feeding the sheep," her mother said.
Snowy day, corn and hay.

"What are you doing?" the little girl asked.

"Shearing the wool," her mother said.
Soft and deep, sheepy heap.

"What are you doing?" the little girl asked.
"Washing the wool," her mother said.
Soap and steam, fleecy clean.

"What are you doing?" the little girl asked.

"Drying the wool," her mother said.
Windy day, wool ballet.

"What are you doing?" the little girl asked.
"Carding the wool," her mother said.
Push and pull, brushes full.

"What are you doing?" the little girl asked.
"Spinning the yarn," her mother said.
Fluffy pile, takes a while.

"What are you doing?" the little girl asked.
"Dyeing the yarn," her mother said.
Deepest blue, messy brew.

"What are you doing?" the little girl asked.
"Knitting the wool," her mother said.
Knit and purl, needles whirl.

"What are you doing?" the little girl asked.
"Keeping you warm," her mother said.
Sweater snug, woolly hug.

"What are you doing?" the mother asked.
"Feeding the sheep," her little girl said.